THE AUCTION

A LADYBOY SURPRISE

SHAE'S T-GIRL ADVENTURES

VICTORIA RUSH

VOLUME ONE

SHAE'S T-GIRL ADVENTURES - BOOK 1

COPYRIGHT

For the uninhibited...

1

———

I'd been looking forward to attending this year's annual LGBT charity fundraiser, not only because it would give me the chance to mingle with many long-lost friends and colleagues, but also rub shoulders with some of the city's most notable celebrities and politicians. The mayor would be there of course, but also plenty of famous athletes, musicians, and movie stars. As I slipped on my clingy silk ball gown and Christian Louboutin heels, I angled my body sideways to examine my figure in my full-length wardrobe mirror.

Not too shabby for a thirty-five-year-old, I nodded to myself.

My natural breasts stood high and plump behind my plunging neckline, and my butt was still round and firm against the outline of my gown. Even my larger-than-normal boy-cock was nicely concealed behind the thigh-high slit of my dress from my tight-fitting compression underwear. I was curvy in all the right places and excited to see who I'd have a chance to meet at the swanky gala. It had been too many weeks since I'd been on a proper date, and I could feel my pussy throbbing at the idea of hobnobbing with all these glamorous guests.

I gently placed my Swarovski pendant around my neck, then glanced down at my glistening cleavage under the bright lighting of my walk-in closet. It was a far cry from a *real* diamond necklace, but something told me not many people would be staring that far up my exposed chest anyway. With flushed cheeks and a wide smile, I headed out the front door of my condo when I received a text notification that my Uber ride had arrived to pick me up.

When I got to the Ritz-Carlton hotel, I walked up the granite entrance steps and noticed a sign in the corner of the lobby pointing toward the gala being hosted in the Grand Ballroom. As I approached the closed doors of the room, I could already hear the buzz from the voices of those who'd arrived early, mixing with the sultry sound of soft jazz emanating over the speakers. I presented my entry pass to the doorman, and he opened the door, waving me in. When I entered the room, my eyes widened at the size of the crowd, with well over a thousand well-dressed guests mingling and laughing in small clusters under the sparkling chandeliers. I felt a little awkward and exposed standing there all by myself, and I grabbed a flute of champagne from the silver tray of a passing waiter, quickly gulping it down.

"Shae!" a familiar voice said as someone caressed her fingers over the small of my back from behind. It was Jade, my friend and occasional lover, who I'd met at one of the cabaret shows I performed in.

"Jade!" I said, turning around to give her a big hug. There weren't many people I'd feel comfortable greeting in such an overt physical way, but I'd had enough hot and heavy makeout sessions with Jade to ease any inhibitions I might otherwise have. "It's so good to see you! How long has it been? It seems like ages–"

"I know," she smiled. "Fortunately, I have a pretty active imagination that allows me to relive our many moments together and remind me of you on lonely nights..."

"Don't get me started," I laughed, crossing my legs uncomfortably. "I'm already having a hard enough time keeping my dick in my pants around all these glamorous celebrities and movie stars."

Jade glanced at the high slit in the side of my dress, peering at the curvature of my exposed thigh protruding from the gap, and grinned.

"Well, if you need any help with that, let me know," she said. "Because it doesn't look like I'd have too much trouble massaging that big thumper of yours if you need some temporary relief. We can steal off to the ladies room for a quickie any time you're ready. I've missed playing with that beautiful joystick of yours. My plastic dildos just haven't been doing the job for me lately."

"Stop already!" I groaned, moving closer to her to hide the growing bulge in the lower part of my dress. "I'm trying to act like a *lady* tonight. I don't want anyone to know that I'm carrying a concealed weapon, at least until later in the evening when I might be lucky enough to catch the eye of one of these superstars."

"Well you're certainly a full-blooded woman as far as *I'm* concerned," Jade smiled, kissing me softly on my cheek. "You just happen to have a little extra equipment that makes you even *more* desirable."

"Thanks, sweetheart," I said, glancing around the room to see if I could recognize anyone else I knew. I immediately noticed the flaming red hair of the emcee at my cabaret revue, Ginger Snaps, standing in a small circle with a few of the other female impersonator performers from my troupe. She motioned for me and Jade to join them, and we ambled over in their direction while I discreetly pressed my flaring prick back between the folds of my dripping pussy.

"Hey beautiful," I said when I reached Ginger's group, giving her two kisses on the cheek. "What brings you to the other side of town? This is a long way from our little cabaret club, both geographically and metaphorically. This isn't exactly our usual type of crowd."

"Are you *kidding* me?" Ginger said, placing her hands on her hips. "This is the biggest LGBT party of the year. I wouldn't miss it for anything!"

I peered toward my troupe of fellow 'Lips' performers, glancing at their over-the-top female impersonator costumes.

"Hey guys," I smiled. "Glad you could make it. Do you remember my friend, Jade? She's been to our shows a couple of times–"

"How could we not recognize the prettiest girl this side of Chicago?" one of the performers with the stage name Lola said, holding out his hand to greet Jade warmly. "But go easy on the 'guys' comments–we're trying to stay in character for the duration of this little shindig."

"No worries," I chuckled. "Your secret is safe with me. I'm sure no one would even suspect you're anything other than the glam queens you already are."

"It's a little harder for us than it is for you," Lola grumbled, nodding toward the rest of the group, who were staring at the wide slit of my skirt that exposed my tall, slender legs. "You've already got most of the natural endowments to create the persona. The *rest* of us have to use lots of strategically placed padding and makeup to look like real women."

"All the endowments except *one*," I laughed, nodding

toward the bulging crotches of my friends. "I still have to conceal certain parts to complete the act."

"It's a *shame* too," one of my other colleagues named Roxy said. "We've seen you undressed. It's too bad you save that pretty poker only for your private affairs. I'm pretty sure I'm not the *only* one of us who's fantasized about jumping into your deep end."

"That's sweet of you to say, Rox," I said with a lopsided smile. "But you know how I don't like to mix business with pleasure. It would ruin the special chemistry between us that makes our show such a big hit."

"I suppose so," Roxy frowned. "Just let us know if you want to branch out sometime..."

"Speaking of branching out," Ginger said, interrupting our awkward conversation. "We're going to be auctioning off some special prizes later in the evening. I don't suppose you'd like to volunteer to be one of the date-for-a-night prizes? It's for a good cause after all–"

"What do you mean, *we*?" I said, peering at her with pinched eyebrows. "Are you one of the *organizers* of this event?"

"I'm the MC," Ginger said, nodding her head. "And you'd be a perfect catch for one of these rich celebrities. It's mostly just for show, anyways. They'd be buying you only for one night, with no strings attached."

"I dunno, Ginger," I said, crossing my arms over my exposed bosom. "It's one thing to vamp it up on stage and quite another to go home with the customers. I've never felt comfortable crossing that line..."

"But I understand you *do* make the occasional exception," Ginger winked, smiling toward Jade. "I imagine it wouldn't be the first admirer you've mixed with outside your professional circle."

"Who I mix with outside of work is *my* business," I said, clasping Jade's hand and moving in front of her to make it clear she was off-limits when discussing my private life.

"It's okay, Shae," Jade smiled, rubbing her hips softly against mine. "Ginger has a point. It would just be an innocent date and nothing more. Plus, you'd be raising money for a good cause. You can walk away any time you wish..."

I paused for a long awkward moment, staring at Ginger and my fellow cabaret performers, feeling uncomfortable and flushed.

"Come on, Shae," Lola smiled. "We know you like to flaunt your stuff. You're a natural at this. Besides, don't you want to know how much you're worth? You could raise *thousands* from a simple date."

I shook my head, exhaling heavily, then the rest of my band encircled me, clasping my hands while they sashayed their hips in synchronization.

"Shae, Shae, Shae!" they chanted in unison.

"Free your mind of doubt and danger," they crooned, reprising the Spice Girls' song 2 Become 1 from our cabaret show. *"Be for real, don't be a stranger..."*

"Fine!" I stammered, laughing out loud with my bandmates. "For one night only, I'll make an exception. But no *sex*. It's just a simple date for a good cause."

Ginger nodded, peering around the room at some of the eligible bachelors eyeing my curvy figure from afar.

"Don't close all your options *too* fast," she smiled. "You never know who might choose you for his date. This could be your chance to really spread your wings–"

"Not to mention a few *other* things," Jade said, noticing just as many women staring in our direction. "It could just as easily be a pretty actress or a glamorous rock star..."

2

———

For the next thirty minutes or so, our group stayed together making small talk, then Ginger excused herself for a moment, and the lights in the room suddenly dimmed. Madonna's anthem song *Vogue* began booming over the speakers, and shortly after, the red velvet curtains covering the stage parted, revealing Ginger prancing onto the grandstand, pausing to make exaggerated poses to the beat of the music.

What are you looking at? Madonna's voice crooned.

Strike a pose

Strike a pose

Vogue (vogue, vogue)

Vogue (vogue, vogue)

Before long, the rest of our group was vamping it up and lip-syncing the words while we danced in unison, swinging our arms around our faces as we mimicked Madonna's famous music video. When the song ended, we all collapsed into each other's arms, laughing uproariously and panting excitedly.

"Good evening, ladies and gentlemen and non-binary

people!" Ginger shouted into her hand-held mic. "Are you having fun tonight?"

A loud roar emanated from the crowd, with many people pumping their fists and flipping up their dresses in proud tribute to their sexual identities. Many guests wore extravagant, colorful costumes highlighting their lesbian, gay, and queer personas, but there were just as many plain-black tuxedos and conservative gowns worn by the more reserved members of the audience, betraying their straight inclinations. But I'd had enough experience with all manner of gender orientations and sexual preferences to know that few people were exclusively at one end or the other of the continuum. When presented with the right opportunity, just about *everybody* was willing to stretch their boundaries when it came to sex.

"Welcome to a special evening of music, mingling, and dancing," Ginger continued addressing the crowd. "Thank you for coming to support a wonderful cause, which is the celebration of our wonderful diversity as a blended commu-nity, from lesbian to gay to trans and bi and beyond. Just remember, sex and gender are two different things. But that doesn't preclude one form from engaging with any form of the *other!*"

Another loud cheer rose from the crowd as many people turned to kiss their partners while clasping their buttocks and other body parts tightly.

"And *yes*," Ginger smiled, winking at some of the tuxe-doed men standing uncomfortably close to the stage. "Even you so-called straight people might be able to get in on the action if you play your cards right tonight. Because we know that no one's *entirely* straight–am I right, my queer friends?"

The crowd roared again, raising their wine glasses over

their heads in acknowledgement of Ginger's unspoken truth.

"But for you *shy* ones," she continued. "We have a special treat for you later on this evening. Before we finish the show, we're going to hold an auction where we'll offer up some of the city's leading luminaries for a one-of-a-kind date with the winning bidders. Who knows what might happen when you mix the right kind of oil and vinegar? You might just create the most delicious salad you've ever tasted!"

While another loud cheer emanated from the crowd, I winced as I glanced sideways at Jade.

"So much for 'no expectations'," I frowned. "The way Ginger's painting the picture, my blind date will expect me to show up *naked!*"

"Don't worry," she said, reaching out to squeeze my hand. "Whatever happens, you can always say no. Just make sure you agree to meet in a public place so you can exit easily when the time arrives."

"Okay," I grumbled, noticing that the rest of my friends had departed the group. I'd been so focused on listening to Ginger's monologue that I didn't notice they'd moved on. But it didn't take long to figure out where they'd gone when she introduced the next phase in the show.

"Enough small talk from me," she announced from the stage. "Are you guys ready to *dance*? Because we've got a special act imported all the way from the Lips Cabaret Club: our very own *Chili Girls!*"

As my fellow troupe of cabaret performers sashayed onto the stage chanting the Village People song YMCA, I stared at Jade with disbelieving eyes.

"They're going on stage *without me!*" I huffed. "We *always* perform our gigs together."

"It looks like Ginger had a different role in mind for you

tonight," Jade said, noticing everybody in the room starting to move their bodies in rhythm to the music. "Don't sweat it, it just frees you up to have your own kind of fun. Come on, let's get down and boogie with the rest of the crowd."

Young man, there's no need to feel down, my bandmates crooned from the stage,

Young man, 'cause you're in a new town, there's no need to be unhappy,

Here's a place you can go when you're short on your dough,

You can stay there and I'm sure you will find many ways to have a good time...

While Jade and I started to swivel our hips and grind our butts together in tandem, I soon forgot about Ginger's snub, concentrating on watching Jade's sexy body writhing to the music. She was wearing a high-cut black Lycra dress that clung to every curve of her body, and it didn't take long for me to begin undressing her with my eyes while I reflected back on our last fling at her place where we scissored our hips together as she pumped my flapping hard-on with her free hands.

I could feel my dick hardening in my panties while I imagined fucking her, watching her squirt all over my pulsating pussy. I was dying to free my throbbing organ and take matters into my own hands, but I dared not remove my bound erection from the confines of my dripping folds, lest I reveal to everyone in the room my hidden secret. I wasn't quite ready to free the beast and show my true colors, at least until I completed my formal duty at the end of the night. Then I'd be free to go home with whomever I wanted and do whatever I pleased, far away from the prying eyes of others.

It's fun to stay at the YMCA, my female impersonator colleagues continued singing from the stage,

You can get yourself clean, you can have a good meal,
You can do whatever you feel...

By the time the song was over, I was drenched in sweat and in danger of leaving a huge wet mark in the middle of my dress from the combination of my leaking tumescent cock and my dripping pussy from fantasizing about Jade.

"Whew!" I said when the music finally stopped. "I need to take a moment to freshen up. All this upbeat music and suggestive lyrics is making me leak in all the wrong places. Nobody's going to want to go on a date with me tonight if I've got a huge stain in the middle of my dress."

"I dunno," Jade grinned. "Maybe that will only make you all the more appealing. They'll just see it as getting yourself already in the mood–"

"That's not the kind of *mood* I'm trying to create," I frowned. "At least until I see who I'm going on a date with and what his or her intentions are. Not everybody is ready to get their freak on with a *ladyboy*."

"I think you're selling yourself short," Jade said. "You've got everything any red-blooded man or woman could possibly want. A body to die for, a gorgeous face, and sex parts for every occasion."

"That's what I'm worried about," I said. "I don't want to give someone a heart attack when they realize they got a lot more than they bargained for."

"I'm sure you'll get a sense for their sexual inclinations over the course of the date. Maybe you can ask some probing questions to hint at their preferences. Have you *ever* taken someone home who didn't eventually warm up to your special charms?"

"Now that you mention it, I don't think so," I nodded softly. "Most people are shocked when they find I'm equipped with a fully functioning penis, but they seem just as intrigued by my equally enticing pussy. I guess I've got enough to satisfy *anyone's* desires..."

"Exactly," Jade smiled. "Do you need some help 'freshening up' in the ladies room? Maybe I can help you relieve some of that pent-up energy you seem to have generated during our last dance."

"As much as I'd love to," I said. "I'm afraid you'd wrinkle a lot more than just my dress. I'd better keep my makeup and hair properly preserved to make a respectable appearance later tonight."

"Suit yourself," Jade said. "Just know that I'm ready and waiting if you want to take a little break."

"Thanks, sweetie," I said, kissing her on the side of her cheek. "Save that thought. Maybe you'll have a chance to win me for the prize later on tonight."

Jade paused as she peered around the room, noticing many of the city's most prominent stars and businessmen.

"I don't think my purse is big enough to keep up with some of these heavyweights," she frowned. "But I'd mortgage my house to have another fling with you in the sack."

"There'll be no need for any of that," I laughed, squeezing her tight ass with my hand. "You can have it for *free* anytime you want."

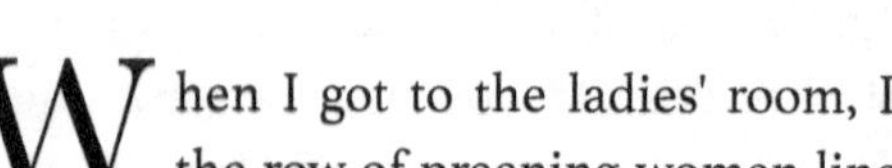

When I got to the ladies' room, I quickly bypassed the row of preening women lined up at the mirror adjusting their makeup and beelined it to one of the vacant stalls. As soon as I closed the door, I yanked down my drenched panties and freed my aching erection as it flipped upward, slapping against my bare belly. I grabbed a clump of toilet paper from the roll on the wall and jerked my dick furiously, cumming hard into the wad while I bit my lip trying to suppress my groans. It wasn't the best sex I'd had in a while, but at least it temporarily relieved the throbbing of my organ and stopped the flood of juices dripping from my pussy.

I dabbed my wet panties as best I could with a fresh wad of TP, then cleaned up the rivulets of lubrication running down the insides of my thighs and angled my softening organ back between my legs, positioning it between the folds of my labia and cinching up my tight panties to keep it secure while carefully taping a mini-pad around the fabric to keep any of the wetness from transferring to my silk gown. When I got up, I straightened the wrinkles in my dress, then nonchalantly walked up to the dressing mirror over the sinks to join the rest of the women to touch up my makeup. Little did they know that a sexy hermaphrodite was standing right next to them with a secret weapon, just waiting to be let loose.

Or maybe they did. Who was to say which of them might also be harboring a hidden secret under their pretty gowns, just like me? If six of my female impersonator friends could pull it off for an entire night under the bright lights of the cabaret stage, why couldn't someone else? After all, this was the biggest LGBT event of the year in Chicago. Surely there were plenty of other transgender people mingling in the crowd, pretending to be someone other than they appeared to be. As I eyed up the attractive women staring into the mirror, my eyes wandered over their sexy bosoms and tight asses, wondering which if any of them might bid for my services later in the evening.

Suddenly, I was feeling a lot more receptive to an anonymous fling with a sexy stranger...

3

───────

When I returned from the ladies room, Jade and I danced for a little while longer, then a few more friends joined us, and I headed over to the bar to grab some drinks. After I placed my order with the bartender, a tall man in a tuxedo ambled up beside me, ordering a Grey Goose martini. He noticed me waiting patiently next to him, then he turned around to face me, peering at the jewel around my neck. I recognized him immediately as the handsome tech tycoon, Aiden Brando, who had a notorious reputation as a serial womanizer, dating everyone from supermodels to famous Hollywood actresses.

"You look a little lonely up here," he said, glancing a little further down my bosom. "Can I get you something to drink?"

"I already placed my order, thanks," I smiled, trying to suppress a blush while I peered into his smoldering eyes.

He was tall and buff in his tailored tux, with a chiseled jaw and glistening lips framing his perfectly straight nose and tanned face. I didn't usually go for this macho type, but there was something about the way he carried himself and the way he stared into my eyes that radiated charisma.

"What brings you out alone to this flashy affair?" he said, raising his martini glass to his lips after the bartender placed it on the counter in front of him. He took a slow, languorous sip, then licked his tongue over his bottom lip to catch a stray drop of vodka.

"I'm–not alone," I stammered, feeling my tool twitching in my panties and pressing against the tight fabric. "I'm with a few friends."

"*LGBT* friends?" he said.

"Some of them," I nodded. "Do you have a problem with that?"

"Of course not," he smiled. "Some of my best friends are lesbian."

"I *bet* they are," I huffed, imagining him surrounded by naked women on his oversize playboy bed.

"What do you mean by that?" he said, placing his martini glass back down on the counter.

"It's just that you have a bit of a reputation as a player. I imagine you like to surround yourself with as many different types of women as possible."

"That's not entirely true," Aiden said. "I enjoy the company of *men* just as much in the right circumstances."

"Are any of them *gay*?" I said, arching an eyebrow.

"Not that I know of," he said, glancing around the room at the diverse crowd. "But you never know, not everyone is open about sharing their hidden secrets."

"Fair enough," I said, watching his arm muscle flex in his tight-fitting tuxedo while he raised his glass once again to his lips. It took everything in my power not to let my eyes stray a little further down to glance at his crotch while he sat on the adjacent stool with his legs splayed apart. "What about *you*? What brings an avowed straight man to an LGBT-themed party like this?"

"Just supporting a good cause," he smiled, peering at me over the rim of his frosted martini glass. "Plus, it's good for business. I try to support *every* demographic. After all, my business is fairly gender-neutral."

"I suppose it is," I smiled as the bartender lined up four cocktails in front of me. "The internet is one of the last remaining bastions of real equality. Anyone can search for any kind of kinky interest with complete impunity."

"I'm not sure my friend Mark Zuckerberg would agree with that," Aiden laughed. "Do you need help carrying those?"

"I can manage on my own, thanks," I said, motioning toward the bartender. "Can you place these on a *tray* so I can bring them to my friends?"

"I'll have a waiter bring them to you in a moment," the bartender nodded. "Just wave your hand over your head when you return to your spot on the floor."

"Thanks," I said, turning back to Aiden. "Enjoy the rest of the show. Perhaps we'll bump into one another again before the evening is over."

"I'll look forward to that," he said, shaking my hand as I stepped off my stool.

Sensing his eyes running up and down the back of my dress, I wriggled my ass like a supermodel while I disappeared into the writhing crowd.

When I reached my friends, I noticed that Ginger and the rest of my troupe had returned, chatting idly with Jade and the others while they awaited my return.

"That took longer than expected," Jade said, peering at me with a worried expression. "Was there a long lineup at the bar?"

"Not for *drinks* so much as for the groupies following that rich tech guy, Aiden Brando," I said.

"You ran into *Aiden Brando* at the bar?" Ginger said, widening her eyes. "Is he as hot in real life as he is on the cover of Vanity Fair?"

"He's alright," I lied. "A bit too arrogant for my liking. You know his type, always looking for another easy conquest–"

"And did you make it *easy* for him?" Ginger grinned.

"He's far too straight and narrow for my tastes," I said, raising my hand in the air when I noticed one of the waiters heading in my direction with a tray of cocktails. "He wouldn't know what to do with my extra equipment."

"I dunno," Lola laughed. "He wouldn't be the *first* guy who'd be happy to find another joystick in the mix. Just say the word whenever you're ready..."

"Speaking of which," I huffed, turning toward Ginger with an angry expression. "I can't believe you invited our cabaret group onto the stage without me! You know we never perform apart!"

Ginger chuckled as she rolled the palm of her hand softly over my bare shoulder.

"I needed you to keep yourself preserved for the prizes at the end of the show. We can't have you getting all hot and sweaty before someone has a chance to choose you for a date."

"Did you ever consider that flaunting my wares on stage might make me more appealing to a wider audience? Showcasing my talent could draw in more bidders..."

"Hmm," Ginger nodded. "You have a point there. We're

getting close to wrapping up. Do you want to join the rest of the group for the final number?"

"I'd love to!" I said, smiling at my bandmates.

"Go backstage and get yourself ready then," Ginger said. "I'll introduce you in a few minutes."

"Just don't break a leg up there," Jade chuckled, kissing me on the cheek before I headed toward the bandstand. "You might need it later on tonight."

"Don't worry," I grinned. "I've got a *third* one if the need should arise."

4

___

After I joined my fellow performers backstage, I added a feathered headdress to my ensemble, then I heard Ginger turning on the mic to address the crowd.

"I hope you've all enjoyed the evening and made lots of new friends at our little shindig," she said. "In the spirit of sharing, we've got one final number to perform before we close the show with some special prizes. Ladies and gentlemen, I give you once again: *the Chili Girls!*"

The red curtains parted and my troupe pranced out onto the stage in a V-formation with me at the front, belting out the LGBT standard, *It's Raining Men.*

We've got news for you, you better listen up, we warbled in unison,

Get ready all you lonely girls,

And leave your umbrellas at home,

'Cause tonight, for the first time in history, it's gonna start raining men.

It's raining men, hallelujah, it's raining men...

The crowd erupted into a loud roar, and suddenly the

sparkling ballroom became a seething mass of moving bodies bumping and grinding into one another. The gender or sexual persuasion of each guest didn't matter, the lyrics resonated equally well with all orientations as gay, lesbian, and trans couples shook their booties and sang along at the top of their lungs. When the song finally ended, you could feel the palpable energy in the room, as everybody cheered wildly, clapping their hands enthusiastically.

Ginger motioned for our troupe to return backstage then the curtain slowly closed and she walked out to the front of the dais.

"Speaking of *raining men*, our next event will showcase a special guest who's generously volunteered his time and services for one very lucky winner. Ladies and gentlemen, may I introduce to you, the two-time Academy Award Winning actor, *Brad Porter*!"

The curtain flapped open, and the crowd oohed and awed as the spotlight shone upon the famous actor, who bowed to the cheering group.

Ginger walked up next to the movie star and shook his hand, pressing the mic up to his lips.

"Thank you for joining us this evening, Brad," she said. "This seems a long way from the Hollywood studios and your live-action films. What brings you to the Windy City to rub shoulders with our diverse crowd?"

"I never miss an opportunity for a good party," Brad smiled, flashing his dazzling teeth.

"Aren't you worried that mingling with all these queer people might damage your *brand*?" Ginger said. "After all, you've got a reputation to uphold, what with all those macho roles you're famous for."

"Well, I am an *actor*, after all," he smiled. "I think I can comport myself respectably enough for one evening in mixed company."

"But what if the winning bidder turns out to be a *man*?" Ginger grinned.

The crowd uttered a long *ooooh*, but he didn't bat an eyelash.

"I guess it depends on the setting and the type of food served over dinner," he grinned, showcasing his famous dimples. "With the right lighting and proper dialog, you can create a good chemistry with *any* willing partner."

The crowd uttered a loud cheer then Ginger moved a few steps to the side, raising the microphone back to her mouth.

"Well there you have it, folks. A leading man looking for his next muse for one special scene with a lucky bidder. Who'd like to start the bidding for a date-for-a-night with one of our greatest actors?"

"One thousand dollars!" a woman's voice blurted from the crowd, holding up a card with her bidding number.

Everyone in the crowd twisted around as the spotlight shone upon the famous singer-songwriter, Taylor Smith, grinning from ear to ear.

"That's a good start," Ginger nodded towards the singer, then she swiveled her head around the crowd. "Surely we can do better than that! I understand that Brad's going rate to headline in a movie starts at *twenty million*. Who wants to raise the bidding?"

"*Two* thousand dollars!" another woman's voice rose from the floor, as the famous actress Jennifer Larson raised her arm.

"That's a little better, but–" Ginger began to say.

"*Twenty* thousand dollars!" the flamboyant gay YouTube

sensation Rock Johnson shouted, pumping up his bidding sign.

Porter shifted uneasily from one foot to the other as he struggled to maintain a strained grin while another loud cheer rose from the crowd.

"*Now* we're starting to get somewhere," Ginger smiled. "But surely one night alone with Brad Porter is worth more than that. Imagine the stories you'll be able to tell your grandchildren one day. And who knows what might happen after you share a few glasses of wine? Maybe Brad will take you on a tour of our fair city in his famous helicopter..."

"One hundred thousand dollars!" another woman's voice called out from the audience, and the spotlight shifted over the crowd until it found a tall blonde woman lifting a card over her head. The bidder was none other than Brad's on-and-off-again girlfriend, Scarlett Soldana, with whom he'd co-starred in a number of romantic movies.

"Awww," Ginger hummed in approval. "This looks like a match made in heaven. Are there any other takers? What do you say, Brad? Does this bidder meet with your approval?"

"I recognize that voice," he nodded. "Something tells me we won't need any special effects or mood music to make this date work. I'm pretty sure I can make it worth her while..."

"It's a date then," Ginger grinned. "You can meet your partner backstage after she presents her pass to make final plans." Then she peered out into the audience, raising an eyebrow to elevate the suspense. "Now, who will be our *next* eligible bachelor or bachelorette to make themselves available for an exciting night of wining and dining?"

Brad walked off the stage, then a sequence of famous male and female celebrities alternately stood in the spotlight while Ginger ribbed them good-naturedly as the audience members bid for their time. After two more men and two women had taken their turn, Ginger motioned for me to get ready to approach the podium. I removed my boa and flattened the wrinkles in my dress while my fellow performers straighten my hair and wished me well.

"Our last prize for the night," Ginger announced over the speakers. "Is someone who has some extraordinary talents, and I don't just mean as a cabaret singer. Please join me in welcoming to the stage, one of our very own Chili Girls – *Shae!*"

I walked out onto the stage unsteadily, trying not to twist my ankles in my high heels while the bright spotlight shone on my glittering dress. I was thankful that the improvised mini-pad had absorbed my previous emissions and that my compression underwear was holding my flaccid prick tightly concealed between the folds of my labia.

Ginger walked up next to me as she had with the other date-for-a-night volunteers and placed her arm around my shoulder.

"Have you got enough energy left for one more act tonight, Shae?" she said, winking at me.

"Anything should be easier than prancing on stage in these high heels," I said, offering a lopsided smile.

"Indeed it should be," Ginger nodded. "Plus, you'll be entertaining someone one-on-one this time, although it will likely be someone you've never met before. Have you ever gone on a date with a *stranger* before?"

"Well, I've been on a date with a few strange *people*, that's for sure..."

The crowd chuckled, then Ginger pressed the microphone closer to my mouth.

"How do you feel about mixing it up with someone from

the *rainbow* community? Where do you place yourself on the continuum?"

I glanced at Ginger with a disapproving stare, angry at her for putting me on the spot so publicly, then I shrugged my shoulders.

"Well, I've always considered myself *pansexual*. The gender and sexual orientation of my partners doesn't matter if I find them attractive and intriguing enough."

"Well said, Shae," Ginger nodded, returning the mic to her mouth. "Who'd like to start the bidding for this talented and sexy performer?"

"Five thousand dollars," a woman's voice called out from the audience, as the spotlight focused on the well-know blonde singer, Adeline.

"Well," Ginger smiled, peering out at the pretty crooner. "The two of you would certainly create some beautiful *harmonies* together, that's for sure–"

"*Ten* thousand," another woman yelled, thrusting her bidding card high in the air.

This time it was the famous actress Kristen Spenser, who'd publicly renounced her leading woman role when she went public as a proud lesbian.

"Mmm," Ginger hummed. "I'd like to be a fly on the wall during *that* little date. I can only imagine the sparks that might fly from that collaboration..."

"Twenty thousand!" a third woman shouted with a slightly deeper voice.

This time it was the famous entrepreneur, Meg Stewart, who'd cashed in her stock options after selling her start-up company, U-bay. I was a little perplexed why it was only *women* who'd bid for my services so far, but it didn't bother me too much, since I'd had plenty of torrid affairs with other girls. Besides, it would probably be safer to go on a blind date with another female, who wouldn't have the same pushy expectations as most men.

"There's someone who has plenty of experience bidding for merchandise," Ginger chuckled, nodding toward the latest bidder. "I don't know if anyone's going to be able to top that–"

"Five *hundred* thousand," a man's deep voice rose from the crowd, slowly raising his tuxedoed arm over his head.

I recognized the voice and his thick mane of hair immediately, as the spotlight moved toward his position near the front of the stage. It was Aiden Brando, the handsome billionaire who'd flirted with me earlier in the evening. I felt my heart suddenly fluttering in my chest and my dick twitching in my underwear, imagining what it would be like to have him alone for an entire evening where I could learn more about his interests and desires.

"Wow!" Ginger exclaimed, widening her eyes as she placed her hand over her eyebrows, peering out at the handsome bidder. "That sets a new record for this evening's bidding. This paramour must see something special in our final candidate. Does anyone want to try topping his bid? Going once, going twice – *sold* to the handsome gentleman in the front row."

~

After the bidding closed for the evening and the curtain closed with Ginger thanking everyone for contributing to the event, I returned backstage to find a huge bouquet of flowers waiting on my dressing room table.

"Looks like you have a secret admirer," Roxy smiled, winking at me teasingly.

"Something tells me he's not so *secret*," Lola laughed,

taking off the last of his makeup in front of the mirror with some alcohol swabs.

"Am I interrupting anything?" a man's voice said as Aiden appeared in the doorway to the dressing room.

"No," Lola smiled. "We were just about to close up shop. We'll leave you two lovebirds to plan your next date."

"Lovebirds?" Aiden said after everyone else left the dressing room. "Aren't we moving a little fast on this blind date thing?"

"They're just acting like their usual prima donnas," I said, chuckling softly. "I wouldn't make too much out of it."

"Your friends sure look a lot different when they take off their *makeup*," Aiden said, sitting next to me on the adjacent dressing room chair. "I hope *you* won't have such a dramatic transformation when you take off your costume. I was kind of getting used to that pretty face and sexy figure."

"Not to worry," I fibbed. "I'm pretty much the same girl under the surface that you see on the outside. Although I'm worried you might have overbid for a single date–"

"How *else* was I going to get you alone?" he said. "You were playing pretty hard to get at the bar."

"That's just because I had to get back to my friends," I said. "Now you've got me all for yourself, at least for one night."

"I like the sound of that," Aiden smiled. "Although the current night is already almost over. How would you feel about starting over this coming Friday? I know a place overlooking the lake with views to die for. And the food is prepared by a personal friend of mine..."

"We are talking a *restaurant*, right?" I said. "Because I'm not quite ready to share a meal with your personal chef at your home."

"Of course. It's called Cindy's on Michigan Avenue. Can I send a car for you at eight p.m.?"

"That would be lovely, thank you," I said.

"It's a date then," Aiden nodded. "I just need one more thing, your phone number. That is, unless you were planning on disappearing into the crowd again..."

"I wouldn't think of it," I laughed, scribbling my number on a piece of paper and handing it to him with an outstretched hand.

"Perfect," he said. "I'm looking forward to seeing you again, Shae. Do you need a drive home?"

"I'm good, thanks," I said. "It's probably best to keep a little distance between us until our formal date. I wouldn't want to create the wrong impression–"

"I don't think there's any danger of that," he smiled. "Although you've certainly raised a lot more than just my *expectations* so far."

"Thank you for the flowers, Aiden. I'm looking forward to seeing more of you also."

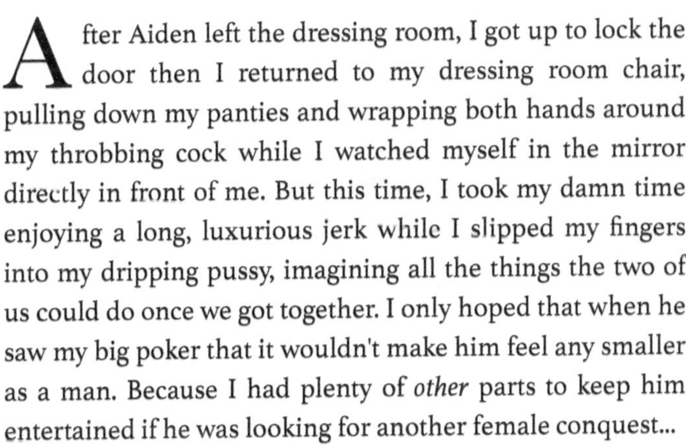

After Aiden left the dressing room, I got up to lock the door then I returned to my dressing room chair, pulling down my panties and wrapping both hands around my throbbing cock while I watched myself in the mirror directly in front of me. But this time, I took my damn time enjoying a long, luxurious jerk while I slipped my fingers into my dripping pussy, imagining all the things the two of us could do once we got together. I only hoped that when he saw my big poker that it wouldn't make him feel any smaller as a man. Because I had plenty of *other* parts to keep him entertained if he was looking for another female conquest...

5

Over the next few days, I was equal parts excited and terrified about my upcoming date with Aiden. Part of me wanted to let him tear off my clothes and take me in his strong arms while he fucked me hard on his king-size bed. But the other part of me was frightened how he would react when he found out that I was more than he expected. He'd dropped enough clues about his attraction to me as a full-blooded woman, and he didn't seem to harbor the slightest gay or bisexual inclination whatsoever. There was no accounting for how he might react when he took off my clothes and discovered a flapping hard-on bouncing over my belly.

No matter, I said to myself while I finished touching up my makeup in preparation for this evening's scheduled pickup. *I'll just play it by ear over dinner and probe around the edges to see what his kinks are. Because everybody's got one predilection or another. If he doesn't bite at my ladyboy hints, I can always keep my pants on and call it a day when the dinner is over.*

Except I wasn't wearing any pants for this date. I'd purposefully chosen a clingy, see-through lace dress with a transparent bra that showed just enough of my medallion-sized nipples under the fabric to keep him focused on my *upper* half while we chatted and ate our food. And this time, instead of wearing tight compression underwear to keep my flaring cock under control, I decided to wear a skimpy thong to showcase my firm ass without any panty lines. I'd just have to keep my mind from wandering under the table during our conversation to keep my thumper from getting any extra ideas. At least until he took me back to his place for an after-dinner nightcap.

I glanced at my phone when it buzzed on the counter next to me and quickly finished putting on my lipstick.

My driver's outside waiting for you, Aiden's text message read. *I'll meet you on the rooftop of the hotel on the thirteenth floor. I've got a private table waiting for us.*

I grabbed my clutch purse and threw in a packet of extra wet wipes just to be safe.

Keep it together, Shae, I said to myself. *It's just a date. Don't get your hopes up—or anything else—until you're good and ready.*

Out on the street, I climbed into the back seat of Aiden's Maybach limousine while the driver held the door open for me, then I stared out the window as the car moved into the upscale part of the city along Michigan Avenue, stopping in front of the Athletic Association Building. It wasn't quite as glamorous as I was expecting, but I stepped out of the car and walked up the steps into the marble-lined foyer, looking for the elevator bank to take me to the 13th floor.

"Lucky thirteen," I said, taking in a deep breath as I pressed the button for the rooftop bar.

When the elevator doors opened, the restaurant maitre d' was waiting for me, and he escorted me through the glass-ceiling atrium to the private terrace overlooking Millenneum Park and Lake Michigan. Adrian stood up from a white-linen-covered table when he saw me, presenting me with a beautiful bouquet of long-stemmed Calla lilies.

"Flowers again?" I said, kissing him on the cheek and blushing softly. "I could get used to this. How did you know these were my favorites?"

"I just had a feeling," he smiled. "Simple, elegant, and gorgeous, just like you."

"I'm not sure about the *simple* part, but I'm happy to accept them," I said, taking a seat at the table while he pulled out my chair.

"Can you put these in a vase for us, Emilio?" Aiden said, peering up at the maitre d' before he went back into the main room of the restaurant.

"Sure thing, Mr. Brando," the maitre d' said.

I peered around the breezy terrace, surprised there was only one table arranged for such a large space.

"Have you got this whole terrace reserved just for *us*?" I said, peering at the pretty whitecaps rolling across the shimmering lake in the distance.

"I didn't want any distractions," he nodded when the maitre d' returned with my flowers in a tall vase, placing it in the center of the table. "People can sometimes be quite rude taking pictures with their mobile phones. I don't want any memes showing up on Facebook before we finish our date."

"Thanks," I said. "I'm not used to being treated like this."

"It helps when you know the right people," Aiden said, winking at the maitre d', who was still hesitating at the edge of our table.

"May I get you some aperitifs to start, sir?" the maitre d' said.

"How about some champagne to kick things off?" Aiden said, smiling across the table at me.

"I never say no to champagne," I smiled.

"Two Camparis with Moet, Emilio," Aiden nodded toward the maitre d'.

"You look beautiful tonight," he said when the maitre d' returned inside. "Even more than at the gala last weekend, if you don't mind my saying."

"It's a little more *revealing*," I blushed, placing my hands in my lap. "Perhaps you're being slightly biased by my other attractions..."

"I like this high-cut choker look on you," he nodded. "It shows off all your curves without the need for any unnecessary jewelry."

"You mean my fake diamond necklace?"

"I hadn't noticed," Aiden said.

"You're a good liar," I chuckled. "But thank you for being discreet about it."

The maitre d' returned with two orange-tinted flutes of champagne, placing each goblet softly in front of our respective place settings.

"To new friends," he said, raising his glass toward me.

"And shiny objects," I smiled, chinking my glass against his while peering down at the glistening chrome sculpture of Cloud Gate by the British artist Anish Kapoor, resting on the manicured grounds of the park.

As the two of us watched the sun setting over the lake during the course of our gourmet meal, Aiden and I grew increasingly bold and adventurous sharing details of our personal and professional lives. When it came time for dessert, a new server came out to our table dressed in a chef's hat with long corkscrew hair bundled up on her head.

"Are you enjoying the meal so far?" she said, smiling at Aiden as if he were a member of the family.

"Yes, Cindy," Aiden said, wiping the corners of his mouth with a linen napkin. "Your dishes are exquisite, as always."

"I'm happy to hear," the executive chef smiled, glancing toward me. "And is your *guest* enjoying the meal as much as you are?"

"I hope so," Aiden said, extending his hand toward me. "This is my date, Shae. I'll let her speak for herself."

"I'm not sure which I'm enjoying more," I said, glancing up at the chef. "The wonderful food, the heavenly view, or the charming company."

"Well, he *is* pretty charming," Cindy smiled. "You better watch out for this one. He'll sweep you off your feet if you're not careful."

"That sounds like fun," I chuckled, grinning toward Aiden. "I might need to lie down pretty soon anyway after all this wine and champagne..."

"Would you like some dessert to stimulate your sweet tooth?" Cindy said. "I've been working on some new creations. I recommend the Black Sesame Pavlova or the Mont Blanc with sweet purple potato cream."

"They both sound irresistible," Aiden said. "What do you say, Shae? Shall we order one of each?"

"Sounds good to me," I nodded, almost wetting my pants at her description of the mouth-watering dishes.

"Enjoy the rest of your evening," the chef said. "I hope to see you both again soon."

After Cindy returned inside to the kitchen, I peered over at Aiden and licked my lips.

"That was the most sensuous description of a food item I've ever heard. I practically came just listening to her describe them."

"I know," Aiden nodded. "She's talented in more ways than one."

"Another one of your personal conquests, perhaps?" I grinned at him.

"I never like to mix business and pleasure," Aiden said. "I'm a part owner of the restaurant."

"I see," I nodded. "I like your credo. I have a similar opinion."

As the candlelight flickered in the gentle breeze of the dimming light, Aiden reached out his palms over the table, and I intertwined my fingers gently with his.

"I've really enjoyed our evening together, Shae," he said. "I don't want to let you slip through my fingers again."

"The evening's not over yet," I smiled. "Maybe if you ply me with enough champagne, you can extend it a little longer."

When the waiter returned with our dessert dishes, we argued briefly over who should have each plate, with Aiden deciding on the fruity meringue and me on the tall vanilla cupcake. As we dug into our respective desserts, we groaned softly at the exquisite taste of the dishes, teasingly spreading the creamy toppings over our pouting lips.

"Would you like to try a bite of mine?" Aiden said, holding his spoon gently in his mouth while he rolled his tongue over the berry-colored fruit.

"I'm kind of enjoying watching you enjoying *yours*," I said. "I like what you're doing with your tongue."

"As am I with yours," he grinned.

"Oh?" I said, sliding the curved underside of my fork up the sides of my cone-shaped torte. "Does this remind you of anything?"

"You mean something tall and pointy that drips cream down its sides when someone caresses it the right way?"

I plucked the cherry off the top of my gateau and sucked it gently between my puckered lips, while Aiden unbuttoned the top of his dress shirt and loosened his tie from his growing distraction.

"Would you like to take a turn caressing my delicacy?" I grinned. "Because I think it's about to overflow any second now..."

"Don't mind if I do," Aiden said, reaching out to slide my plate toward him.

But instead of using his spoon to sample the creamy icing, he slid the side of his middle finger up one side of the torte, raising it toward his mouth and licking the cream slowly.

"It looks like you've had some practice doing that sort of thing before," I chuckled. "Do you *enjoy* stroking other people's ganaches?"

"It depends on who's on the other end of the treat. You know what they say: variety is the spice of life."

"Exactly what I was thinking," I said, feeling my panther poking out of my thong and sliding up the side of my thigh under the table. "Do you want to continue this somewhere more private?"

"I thought you'd never ask," Aiden said, standing up with a prominent bulge in the crotch of his trousers while he held out his hand for me.

I hesitated for a moment, staying seated while I crossed my legs to keep my hard-on from tenting my dress any further.

"Do you mind if I take a moment to freshen up in the ladies room first?" I said. "All this messy dessert is ruining my make-up."

"Of course," Aiden said, motioning for the maitre d' to bring him the check.

While he pulled out his Amex card and glanced at the bill, I stood up with my purse in front of my crotch and headed in the direction of the ladies room, trying my best to ignore the throbbing instrument wagging between my legs. When I reached the restroom, I went into one of the stalls, heaving gently while I tried to catch my breath. I was tempted to pull off another quickie to settle my impatient dick, but after a few minutes, my erection began to settle down, and I wiped off the precum dripping out of the tip and curved it back under my folds, pulling my thong over it to hold it secure. When I exited the stall to check myself out in the mirror, thankfully everything looked properly hidden back in place, and I spritzed some perfume over my shoulders before walking back into the main lounge.

"Everything alright?" Aiden said to me as he waited by the reception desk.

"More than alright," I smiled. "I was just thinking about erupting cupcakes and cherry pies."

"That makes *two* of us," Aiden said, grabbing my hand and practically dragging me toward the elevator.

6

———

When we pulled up in front of Aiden's mansion on the North Shore of Chicago, he escorted me through the large double entryway, removing my coat and placing it in the closet opposite the vestibule.

"Would you like something to drink?" he said.

"I better not," I chuckled. "I can barely stand up as it is."

"Why don't we rest on the sofa then?" he said, motioning toward his giant sectional lounge overlooking the lake through his floor-to-ceiling living room windows.

"Wow," I said, taking a seat on the corner cushion, peering out at the moonlit waves. "This is even more beautiful than the view from the restaurant terrace."

"Not as beautiful as *you*," Aiden said, stretching out his hand and clasping mine gently as he sidled up next to me on the sofa.

"Oh Aid—"

He leaned over and kissed me softly on my lips, and I pressed my tongue into his mouth, moaning softly. He ran his fingers through my hair and pulled me closer, intermingling his tongue with mine as he traced one hand down the side of my arm. I was worried that he might feel my hardening cock under my dress and I pulled away briefly, staring into his dark eyes.

"Do you mind if we go to your bedroom for a bit more privacy?" I said, glancing out the windows. "I'm feeling a little shy, exposed like this in front of all these windows."

"Of course," he said, standing up and taking my hand as he escorted me toward the master bedroom.

I was happy that he walked a couple of steps ahead of me as he pulled me toward the boudoir, so as not to notice the raging bulge in my panties. When we got to his bedroom, he went to the window to pull the curtains shut, then he returned in the near-darkness to the side of the bed where I'd angled my body toward the pillows. He ran his hands up the center of my back until he found the top of my zipper, then he slowly pulled it down over the curvature of my ass, cupping his hands softly over my buttocks. I heaved my chest in excitement and he deftly unclasped the back of my bra, sliding my dress down onto the floor. I lay on his bed with my back angled toward him, and he kicked off his shoes, holding me from behind. His hand curled around the nape of my neck, caressing the front of my throat, then his fingers traced a line down to my hardening nipples, rolling them between his fingers. I moaned softly, arching my back to meet his touch as my swelling organ slipped out of my panties, angling up toward my stomach.

"Aiden," I said, trying to give him fair warning. "There's something I should tell you–"

"It's alright," he whispered, sensing what I was about to say. "It doesn't bother me if you're having your period..."

"No, it's not that," I said as his palms slid down the front of my stomach until his hand bumped against the tip of my dripping hard-on.

"What the–?" he said, suddenly jerking upright on the bed. "What the hell is *that*?"

"I was trying to tell you–"

"You're a *tranny*?" he said, glaring at me with pointed brows.

"No," I said, grimacing at his use of the pejorative term. "I was *born* this way. I believe the scientific word is hermaphrodite, but prefer the term intersex. I've got a mish-mash of chromosomes, mostly female. I was just born with a fully formed penis."

Aiden stared down at my crotch as I turned around to face him with my throbbing erection bouncing up over my navel.

"No kidding," he said, darting his eyes over the rest of my perineum. "But you've also got a vagina..."

"Yes, and a uterus, though not a fully functioning one since I don't have any ovaries, or *testes*, as you can see. Which is kind of a blessing, since I never get a period, nor can I get pregnant."

"This is a lot to take in," Aiden said, sighing heavily as he leaned back on outstretched arms.

I gritted my teeth, trying to hold back the tears beginning to well up in my eyes.

"You don't find me *attractive* anymore?" I said.

Aiden raised his head and looked at me with a pained expression.

"No, I still find you incredibly beautiful," he said. "It's just that I had no idea–"

"I'm still a lady in every *other* possible way," I said, forcing a smile.

"I know," he said, darting his eyes over my upturned

breasts and curvy hips as he shifted uncomfortably on the bed next to me.

I glanced down at the crotch of his trousers, noticing a prominent bulge still in his pants, and smiled.

"Touch me," I said, sensing his interest in me as something more than just a sideshow.

He paused for a moment then he reached out his hand, running them softly over one of my breasts, caressing my erect nipples with the back of his fingers.

"Their *magnificent*," he said, sliding his hand softly around the underside of my breasts.

"I like the way you touch them," I sighed, arching my back in pleasure. "You seem to know your way around a woman's body."

"Not one like this," he said, his cheeks becoming flushed as he hesitated to move his hands lower.

"Go ahead," I said, sensing his apprehension. "Touch me everywhere."

"But I've never touched a man's – or *anyone's* – hard cock before."

"I imagine you've touched your *own* enough times," I smiled. "It's not so different. Kind of like riding a bike, I imagine."

"A much *larger* bike," Aiden said, drifting his hand down the middle of my stomach toward my flapping organ.

"Yes," I hissed when his hand slid across my swelling glans. "Caress it like you caress your own cock."

He shifted his body closer in my direction, then he circled his fingers around the shaft of my organ, squeezing it firmly.

"My God, Shae," he said, widening his eyes. "It's huge."

"You have that effect on me," I said. "It's been supremely

difficult to keep it under wraps all this time that I've been with you."

"You might have *told* me," he said, squeezing my bulbous crown between his thumb and his forefinger as if to test if my phallus was real.

"I tried to a couple of times," I said. "With those comments over dinner, and your seeing that I was part of a female impersonator troupe..."

"Except you're not at all like them," Aiden said, sliding his hand down my throbbing cock until he found my dripping slit, slipping two fingers into my crevasse.

"Uhnnn," I groaned, rocking my hips softly against his fingers. "That feels good–"

"But I don't see a clit..."

"A woman's clit extends far beyond what you normally see on the outside," I said. "I have sensitive erectile tissue surrounding the entire inside surface of my vagina. It feels good no matter which way you touch me."

"Holy shit," Aiden said, staring at my prick bouncing against my stomach while he fingered my pussy with his fingers. "I'm starting to feel a little inadequate around you. You're like some kind of *super* woman."

"That's sweet of you to say," I smiled, reaching out to unbuckle his pants. "But I've seen enough of you to know that you're more than enough man for me. Let me get these trousers off you so I can play with your dessert at the same time."

"You better be careful, lest it erupt all over your hands," Aiden said. "I wouldn't want to make a mess of your make-up."

"In this case, I'll only be too happy for you to mess my make-up. Because I plan on sucking on a lot more than just the *cherry* on top..."

7

I quickly unbuckled Aiden's trousers and unzipped his fly, pulling his pants down over his legs and tearing off his underwear. Then I shimmied my hips up toward his, placing our upturned poles against one another while we kissed each other passionately.

"See?" I moaned into his mouth. "It seems that we're a pretty good match, after all."

He slid his fingers down over my chest, cupping my tits firmly in his hands while he humped my hips, breathing heavily on my face.

"Fuck, you're hot," he groaned. "This is insane!"

"Are you warming up to my little accoutrements?" I smiled as he stared down between our legs, watching our hard-ons sliding together between our bellies.

"Yes," he panted. "Although I'd say it's far from *little*."

"I dunno," I said, leaning backward and sliding my hands between our stomachs as I wrapped my fingers tightly around both of our dicks. "Yours is just as thick, and almost as long. This will do just fine satisfying my needs."

"That feels *incredible*," Aiden moaned, watching me jerk our two cocks together.

"Maybe you should try this more often," I chuckled, sliding my thumb over his glistening tip and watching his precum roll over his crown. "There's a wide world of diverse pleasures out there, with people of every sexual and gender persuasion."

"I'll stick with girls for now," Aiden huffed, interlacing his fingers with mine while humping his cock harder against mine. "Or at least ladyboys like you."

"*Intersex*, remember?" I reminded him. "Most ladyboys are just men transitioning to female or other non-binary roles. You won't find many with both male and female authentic parts."

"I'll keep that in mind," Aiden grunted, kissing me harder while he squeezed our pricks together. "But I don't have any interest in testing the limits of the gender continuum any further. Can I just call you *Shae* for now?"

"I'd like that," I said, feeling his slippery dew spilling down both sides of our hands. "But I want to feel you coming *inside* me this first time."

I leaned my body forward and raised up on my knees, temporarily pulling our dicks apart, then I angled my pussy over the tip of his dripping organ, sliding myself slowly down the length of his erection.

"Oh my God, Shae," he groaned in ecstasy. "You're so tight and wet."

"That's what you do to me," I purred. "Pretty much from the first time we met."

"Even when you were playing coy with me at the bar during the gala?"

"*Especially* then," I smiled. "I wanted to get in your pants ever since you told me you enjoy the company of men as much as women."

"I meant in the business sense–"

"I figured as much," I said, feeling my erection slapping against our bellies while he held me tightly on his lap. "Have you changed your mind since then?"

"I still like girls," he said, digging his fingernails into the back of my ass. "I mean *women*. Or *ladyboys*. Or inter–"

"Don't sweat it, babe," I chuckled, thrusting my tongue deep into his mouth. "Just fuck me with that thumper and make me come. I'm going to squirt any moment all over your chest..."

"You mean with your cock?" he said, peering down at my prick bouncing between our rocking bodies.

"Yes," I grunted. "Even though you're fucking my pussy, I can feel the pleasurable sensations emanating all the way up to my penis. It's really just an oversize clit, after all."

"Can I *feel* it when you come?" Aiden said, placing his hands between our stomachs to grip my swelling organ with both hands.

"Yes," I groaned, feeling my orgasm rapidly building up in my hips. "If you jerk it at the same time, it feels even better."

Aiden wasted no time flapping his hands up and down over my throbbing shaft while I rode him like a horse, bucking my hips wildly against his thighs.

"Fuck, yes," I growled. "Squeeze my dick harder. I'm going to come so hard. Come with me babe..."

"Oh God, oh God," Aiden huffed, sucking my nipples into his mouth as his face reddened approaching the most intense orgasm of his life.

"*Nnnngah!*" he gasped, pulling me down hard over his hips while he shot his cum deep inside my cavity.

When I felt him climaxing, I tightened my legs around the back of his buttocks, then I shot a huge load of spunk high over our bellies, splashing against the front of our chests and mashing faces. Aiden didn't let go of me until I finished twitching against his stomach, pressing his lips tightly against mine while he groaned like a wounded animal. When we finally separated, we both exhaled heavily, staring into each other's eyes with huge smiles on our faces.

"Still think queer sex is just for *freaks*?" I panted.

"You're not a freak," he smiled. "And this doesn't feel *queer*. You're an extraordinary woman, Shae."

"Does this mean our little transaction isn't finished yet?" I grinned. "Because I can think of a million other ways I want to make love to you."

"I can't wait to try," Aiden said. "After all, that was a pretty large sum I paid for you. I plan on getting the maximum return on my investment."

8

———————

"**O**kay," I smiled at Aiden. "You purchased me for the night, so what would you like to try now?"

"I dunno," he said, staring at my dripping, still tumescent cock. "I can't take my eyes off your dick. There's something about a pretty girl with a big hard-on that's hot as fuck."

"Maybe you have more gay inclinations than you thought," I grinned, noticing his organ twitching while he stared at my tool. "Have you ever had any fantasies that you wanted to try?"

Aiden paused for a moment, then he smiled sheepishly at me.

"Well, I always wondered what it would feel like to suck another man's cock..."

"Well, here's your big chance," I grinned. "In the privacy of your own home, with a *girl* attached. Do you want to give it a try?"

"Are you ready to do it again already?" Aiden said, pinching his eyebrows. "Normally, most guys need a little recovery time before they can get it up again."

"That's the beauty of having a cock with no *balls*," I said. "I don't have to wait for my sperm to regenerate to get back in the mood. That's another way I'm more like a woman. I can have multiple orgasms with near impunity."

"And yet I noticed you squirt *semen* during our last encounter. Where does that come from, if you don't have any testes?"

I nodded my head, recognizing the familiar look of confusion on Aiden's face. This wasn't the first sexual partner I'd had to explain my unusual configuration to, and it wouldn't be the last.

"I still have a prostate gland," I said. "Or something akin to it. As do most other women, for that matter. Theirs is called the *Skene's Gland*, located just behind the G -spot, and it serves a similar function, to facilitate the transportation of sperm up the vaginal canal toward the uterus and ovaries."

"Except you don't have any ovaries..."

"Lucky me," I chuckled. "I guess something got lost in the mixing up of my parents' genes. There'll be no babies for me."

"Does that *bother* you?" Aiden said, nestling up closer to me. "I mean as a person with mostly feminine traits, do you miss that part of the female experience?"

"Not really," I said. "I made peace with it a long time ago. Around the same time I knew I couldn't menstruate."

"What about your *sex organs*?" Aiden said, peering down at my glistening slit and bobbing pole. "Which one do you normally like to play with when you're feeling horny and alone? Your cock or your pussy?"

"They *both* feel good to stimulate," I smiled. "Although I find it's more fun to watch my hard-on when I play with myself."

Suddenly, Aiden's dick bounced upward, and he looked at me with wide eyes.

"Would you mind if I watched while you do that? I mean, if you're still in the mood..."

"Oh, I'm in the mood alright," I grinned. "But only if you do it *together* with me. I want to see how you like to be stroked so I can, um–*maximize your return*."

"You're twisting my arm," Aiden chuckled, rolling his dripping crown between his fingers.

"Come sit beside me against the headboard," I said, propping up his pillows and patting the mattress next to the top of the bed. "We can try some oral *play* a little bit later if you're still in the mood."

"Okay," Aiden said, shifting his body towards the head of the bed and taking off his shirt and tie, throwing them onto the floor next to my dress.

I sat next to him and placed my left leg over his right knee as he spread his legs apart while staring down at the glistening folds beneath my upturned phallus.

"God, even your *pussy* is beautiful," he panted, taking hold of his now fully erect cock with both hands.

"Do you *like* it when I touch myself there?" I said, sliding my hands over my shaved mound and slipping my fingers into my slippery slit.

"Fuck, yes," Aiden grunted, starting to jerk his cock harder. "I've never been so turned on watching a woman masturbate before."

"That's probably because you've never seen one with *both* sets of the equipment," I shuddered, grabbing the crown of my dick with one hand while thrusting three fingers of my other hand deep into my throbbing hole.

"Jesus, Shae," Aiden gasped, as his mouth yawned open in deepening pleasure. "You are one lucky lottery winner.

What I'd do to have two sets of functioning sex organs. It must feel incredible–"

"Careful, cowboy," I chuckled. "You're starting to reveal your true stripes. You wouldn't want your bisexual fantasies to get out into the open where they could damage your reputation as the city's most eligible straight bachelor."

"My secret will be safe with you," he smiled. "As long as you promise to keep it behind closed doors."

"I wouldn't dream of sharing your secret," I said. "As long as you save your kinky desires for me."

"I'm not sure I could go back to a normal woman even if I *tried* after this," he grunted. "You've spoiled me with your incredible beauty and a body to die for."

"Don't die just yet," I rasped, jerking my hard-on in synchronicity with his while I slapped my palm against my wet perineum, burying my fingers deep inside my dripping pussy. "Because I'm not finished with you yet."

"Neither am I," Aiden said, suddenly pulling his hands off his flushing dick and bending over to lower his mouth toward my crotch.

When he took my throbbing crown into his mouth and started sucking it like he was inhaling a thick milkshake, I spread my legs further apart and placed my hands over the back of his scalp. Aiden was more skilled that I imagined he'd be sucking a cock for the first time, twirling his tongue around the underside of my coronal ridge while popping his head up and down over my glans and gripping my thick shaft with two hands.

Or maybe he'd just had plenty of practice getting blown by a succession of pretty *supermodels*, knowing exactly what he liked himself. Either way, I was in heaven while he knelt between my legs and worshipped my throbbing organ. I could see his hard-on flapping between his legs while he rocked back and forth, and for a brief moment I considered pushing him onto his back so I could return the favor. But as I began to feel the familiar pangs of an impending climax building up deep within my crotch, I decided to let him have his way with me for now and enjoy my orgasm. He was like a little boy who'd just been given his favorite toy for Christmas, obsessed with playing with it every way he could before the novelty wore off. As I watched him humming away happily while he bobbed his head over my swelling dick, I thought I should give him fair warning before I shot my load down his throat.

"Aiden, that feels so good," I panted, feeling myself approaching the point of no return. "I'm going to come soon. Oh fuck, I'm going to come so hard–"

He nodded his head and increased the ferocity of his sucking, lowering his head even further down my pole as he took more of my instrument into his mouth. When I couldn't hold it any longer, I grabbed both of his ears and locked his head over my exploding erection, humping my hips against his face while I emptied my load in powerful contractions down his throat. It seemed to take almost a full minute for me to stop pulsing and contracting in his mouth, and I worried that he wouldn't be able to take my full load without gagging or coming up for air. But he swallowed everything like a champ and waited for me to stop moving before he slowly raised his head and peered at me with a Cheshire Cat grin.

"Holy fuck, Aiden," I panted. "For a guy who professes to have never given a person a blowjob before, you sure as hell know how to suck a cock. That's the best head I've had in a long time, from either a man or a woman."

"I'm glad you liked it," he smiled, wiping the last traces of cum from the sides of his mouth. "I guess I have a pretty active imagination. I always wondered what this would feel like from the other end."

"You didn't mind me coming in your mouth?"

"Not at all," Aiden said. "It didn't taste nearly as bad as I imagined. It was kind of *sweet* actually..."

"Like my lava cake at the restaurant?" I smiled.

"Even better," he grinned. "Because you were able to enjoy it equally as much at the same time."

9

———

I peered down at Aiden's cock, which was still bobbing up over his stomach, and smiled.

"It looks like you're still in the mood for a little more action. Are you hard enough to try something *else*?"

"Are you *kidding* me?" Aiden said. "I haven't been this hard since I was fourteen and saw my first naked woman on one of those porn sites."

"What did you have in mind?" I said. "Perhaps you'd like me to return the favor? I know what guys like, having had plenty of experience on the receiving end..."

"Maybe later," Aiden nodded. "I want to see *all* of you when I make love to you this time."

"What exactly did you have in mind?" I said, squinting my eyes.

"Can you lie down and turn sideways on the bed?" Aiden grinned, running his eyes up and down the full length of my body. "I want to fuck you in the scissor position."

"That sounds interesting," I said, shaking my head. "That's something only my *girlfriends* seem interested in doing."

"Except this time, I'll be *penetrating* you," Aiden smiled.

He pulled my knees gently apart then he kneeled between my splayed legs, angling his bobbing cock toward my glistening slit. When I felt his tip entering me, I groaned in pleasure, feeling him squeeze the back of my ass.

"Fuck yes," I moaned. "I can see your abs flexing while you hump me."

"And I can see your *prick* bouncing," he grinned.

"You're right," I smiled up at him. "This is pretty hot, being able to watch everything in this position. I'll have to tell my girlfriends to use a strap-on *dildo* the next time they're fucking me this way."

"That's assuming I'm going to *let* you go back to fucking women after this," Aiden said. "Maybe I'll keep you for *myself* from now on–"

"Just to use me for sex?" I teased, sliding my hand around the back of my ass and cupping his balls gently.

"I'm feeling drawn to you in more ways than one," Aiden groaned, leaning forward to kiss me. "You're an extraordinary woman, Shae."

As he kissed me and moaned into my mouth, I played with his balls while he squeezed my breasts and rocked his body slowly against mine. I didn't want this moment of tenderness to ever end, but as I felt his breathing becoming more ragged and the pace of his rocking beginning to increase, I squeezed his balls tighter.

"Come in my pussy, Aiden," I hummed in his ear. "I'm going to squirt all over your belly again."

"Mm-hmm," Aiden groaned into my mouth, tensing his body as he made one final thrust deep inside me, pulsing his dick against the walls of my tunnel.

When I felt him coming, my pussy clamped down on his dick, and at the same time, my hard-on began flexing between our stomachs as it jetted long streams of cum over our heaving chests and flushed faces. But this time, Aiden didn't pull out when we finished coming, sliding down onto the bed next to me and holding me close while we continued kissing and panting in each other's mouths.

"That was incredible," I said, opening my eyes while he peered back at me.

"Just when I thought it couldn't get any better," he nodded. "I haven't come that hard for as long as I can remember."

"It's probably just the novelty of being with a ladyboy for the first time," I chuckled. "I'm sure you'll get tired of me soon enough, like all your other conquests."

"You're not a *conquest*," he said, pulling his head back a few inches to peer at me with a disapproving stare.

"Even though you *paid* to be with me?" I chuckled.

"That's the first time I've ever paid to be with a woman," he said. "And that was only because I found you utterly irresistible."

I paused for a moment, darting my eyes over Aiden's face, trying to divine his intentions.

"What was it exactly that attracted you to me?" I said. "I mean, you couldn't have known that I was a *ladyboy* until you saw me naked..."

"Maybe it was the way you played hard to get with me at the bar at the gala," he said. "I've never had a woman resist my charms quite so easily before. Or maybe it was the way you shook your bootie up on the stage with your fellow performers. Or maybe it was the cheeky attitude you displayed while you were being interviewed by the MC during the bidding process."

"That was an insane price you paid for me," I said. "I was

afraid you were going to lose to that other rich business-woman, Meg Stewart."

"She knew she couldn't keep up with me," Aiden said. "I would have paid almost *anything* to take you home with me."

"So you were planning on this being more than just an innocent date all along?" I grinned.

"If you were willing," he nodded. "I wasn't going to force myself upon you. But when you started playing with your dessert that way and sucking the cherry into your mouth, I knew there was no way I could let you go home alone."

"So what happens *now*?" I said, feeling his semen dribbling out of my pussy while my hard-on began softening and rested against his belly.

"Well, I'd say your debt is more than fully repaid," he smiled. "But I don't want you to leave. Will you spend the night and sleep with me overnight? I'm in no hurry to see you go..."

"Yes," I said, pulling him closer as I kissed him softly on his lips. I had no idea where this strange union was going, but the pounding of my heart told me our connection was something more than just physical...

10

When I woke up the following morning, Aiden wasn't lying beside me, and I frowned, wondering if the glow of our fledgling romance had already begun to wear off. But when I smelled the aroma of freshly baked bacon drifting from the kitchen, I wandered into the living room wearing his white dress shirt, noticing him standing in front of his stove in his boxer briefs.

"Mmm," I said, sidling up next to him and wrapping my arms around his waist. "That smells heavenly."

"I thought you might be hungry after all the exercise we had last night," he smiled, turning around to kiss me softly on my lips. "I know I am."

"I'm hungry for a lot more than just *food*," I grinned, reaching into his briefs to squeeze his dick.

"There'll be plenty of time for that after breakfast," he said, pulling my hand away. "Are you *always* this horny?"

"Only when I'm sleeping next to a skilled lover like you," I grinned.

"Maybe it's because you've got twice as many *sex* organs," he chuckled, reaching under my shirt and playing with my hardening tool.

"Well, you *do* know how to please me in both places," I smiled. "Can you blame me for feeling a little distracted this morning?"

"Perhaps not," he said, slapping me playfully on my ass.

"Can I help you with anything?" I said, peering at the two pans sizzling over his gourmet range.

"I'm almost finished," he said. "If you like salsa with your omelette, you can find some on the inside shelf of the fridge, and there's some chili peppers on the spice rack in the upper cupboard."

"I think I'll have a little of both," I nodded, swinging open the doors of his double-sided Sub-Zero fridge. "Like you said—variety is the spice of life."

I placed the condiments on his big table overlooking the lake next to our pre-made place settings, then Aiden flipped the food onto separate plates, carrying the steaming dishes to the table.

"For you, my lady," he said, placing one of the plates down next to the end chair facing the windows.

"You'll have to stop spoiling me like this," I smiled, inhaling the scent of the food into my lungs while sprinkling some chili peppers over my omelette. "Otherwise, you might have trouble kicking me out of your big mansion of yours."

"I don't have any intention on doing so," he said, raising a strip of bacon to his mouth and sucking on it teasingly. "You're welcome to stay as long as you want."

"Aren't you worried about what your neighbors might say when they see that you're shacking up with a *ladyboy*?"

"It's none of their business what I do in my private life,"

he said. "And besides, nobody would ever guess. You're the most beautiful woman I've ever been with."

"That's very generous of you to say," I smiled with a flush on my face. "But there are a few other people who know my little secret. It's bound to get out there, eventually."

"So what if it does?" Aiden said. "It's twenty twenty-four. People are a lot more open-minded about gender identities and sexual preferences these days. Like the lady at the ball said, everyone's somewhere on the continuum. No one's entirely straight anymore."

"Perhaps not," I said. "But people are quick to judge. You've got a reputation to uphold–"

"*Fuck* my reputation," Aiden said. "I'm rich enough that I can do whatever I want with my time and spend it with whomever I please."

"Okay," I shrugged. "I just don't want you to feel any obligation after sleeping with me last night."

"I plan on doing a lot more than *sleeping* with you," he said, peering out onto his patio at the large infinity pool overlooking the lake. "How would you like to go for a swim after breakfast then take a ride in my catamaran up to Sheboygan?"

"That sounds like fun," I said, dipping my spoon into the jar of salsa and licking it sensuously. "But I'm interested in riding something *else* if you want to try putting this sauce to better use..."

"Oh?" Aiden said, suddenly shifting distractedly in his chair on the opposite side of the table. "What exactly did you have in mind?"

"I've been dreaming about licking your pole all morning," I smiled. "This might add a little extra zest to the experience..."

"Mmm," Aiden grinned. "Bring an extra bottle. I'm thinking of a few ways I'd like to lick it off *your* body also."

Aiden and I pushed our chairs away from the table, then we skipped out onto the pool patio holding hands, flopping onto one of the oversize padded lounge chairs while spreading the salsa sauce over our bodies like giggling children. I lowered my head over his bobbing erection, sucking the tangy dressing down my throat as he simultaneously smeared the sauce over my breasts, hungrily sucking my hard-as-a-bullet teats while I slapped my hard-on against the back of his head. I could feel Aiden's breathing becoming raspy again as he humped my face eagerly, then he suddenly pulled away, raising me up off the lounge chair in his arms. I looked at him with a puzzled expression, and he playfully threw me into the deep end of the pool, jumping in naked after me. I opened my eyes underwater, noticing him swimming toward me, and I kicked my legs hard, gliding under the water as my now fully-erect cock waggled between my legs like a fishing lure. He took me in his arms and we rose to the surface, gasping for air while he pressed me against the side of the pool. I circled my arms around his hips and he seamlessly entered me while I rubbed my cock against his firm abdomen. Within minutes, both of us were shaking and grunting in each other's arms once again, holding each other close and kissing like it was the last day of our lives.

But something told me this was just the beginning of our torrid affair, and as we bobbed our bodies together softly in the rolling water, I closed my eyes, wondering if this was all just a dream...

~

Ready for more ladyboy chills and thrills? Read the next volume in Shae's T-Girl Adventures: Hot Tub Hotel. Buy direct and save at victoriarusherotica.com. Or download from your favorite online bookstore here: retailer links.

Sometimes the most interesting discoveries are found under the surface...

ALSO BY VICTORIA RUSH

Adult Fairytales:

The Enchanted Forest: An Erotic Fairytale

The Land of Giants: An Erotic Fairytale

The Dragon's Lair: An Erotic Fairytale

Witch's Brew: An Erotic Fairytale

The Mage's Spell: An Erotic Fairytale

The Mermaid Lagoon: An Erotic Fairytale

The Coven: An Erotic Fairytale

Rapunzel: An Erotic Fairytale

The Seven Dwarfs: An Erotic Fairytale

The Land of Mutants: An Erotic Fairytale

The Erotic Temple: A Sexy Fairytale (Coming Soon)

Erotica Themed Bundles:

Voyeur: Lesbian Erotica Bundle

Public Affairs: A Lesbian Anthology

Futa Fantasies: The Ladyboy Collection

Threesomes: The Lesbian Collection

Threesomes - Volume 2: The Lesbian Collection

First Time: A Lesbian Anthology

Hedonism: An Erotic Anthology

Switch Hitters: Bisexual Erotica

Taboo Erotica: The Lesbian Series

BDSM: The Lesbian Collection

Party Games: The Erotic Collection

Party Games 2: The Erotic Collection

All Girl 1: Lesbian Erotica Bundle

All Girl 2: Lesbian Erotica Bundle

All Girl 3: Lesbian Erotica Bundle

All Girl 4: Lesbian Erotica Bundle

Erotic Fairytale Bundles:

Clover's Fantasy Adventures: Books 1 - 5

Clover's Fantasy Adventures: Books 6 - 10

Erotic Fantasy:

Pirate's Bounty: A Time Travel Adventure

Wild West: A Time Travel Adventure

Private Riley: A Time Travel Adventure

Cleopatra's Secret: A Time Travel Adventure

Bounty Hunter 2125: A Time Travel Adventure

Ninja Assassin: A Time Travel Adventure

The 300: A Time Travel Adventure

Arabian Nights: An Erotic Fairytale (coming soon...)

Steamy Time Travel Bundles:

Riley's Time Travel Adventures: Books 1 - 5

Lesbian Erotica:

The Dinner Party: Lesbian Voyeur Erotica

The Darkroom: Bisexual Voyeur Erotica

Naked Yoga: Lesbian Transgender Erotica

Nude Cruise: Bisexual Voyeur Erotica

Rush Hour: Taboo Public Sex

The Girl Next Door: First Time Lesbian Erotic Romance

Girls' Camp: Lesbian Group Sex

Wet Dream: Ladyboy Fantasy Erotica

The Convent: Taboo Sex with a Nun

Sex Robot: A Dream Sex Machine

The Personal Trainer: Getting Pumped at the Gym

The Dominatrix: BDSM Lesbian Domination

Webcam Chat: Lesbian Online Sex

Paint Me: A Kinky Bodypainting Workshop

The Toy Party: Girls Sharing Sex Toys

The Costume Party: Strapping One On

Swedish Sauna: Lesbian Group Sex

The Therapist: Taboo Lesbian Erotica

Elevator Shaft: Bisexual Threesomes Erotica

Ladyboy: Lesbian Transgender Erotica

Peep Show: Lesbian Voyeur Erotica

The Dare: Public Sex Erotica

Maid Service: Lesbian Threesomes Erotica

The Hitchhiker: First Time Lesbian Erotica

The Housesitter: Spycam Lesbian Erotica

The Spa: Lesbian Group Orgy

Parlor Games: Blindfold Sex Party

The Exchange Student: First Time Lesbian Erotica

The Hostel: Bisexual Group Erotica

The Harem: Lesbian Erotic Romance

The Orient Express: Lesbian Voyeur Erotica

The First Lady: A Forbidden Lesbian Erotic Romance

The Slave: Lesbian BDSM Erotica

The Masseuse: Lesbian Sensuous Erotica

Too Close for Comfort: Lesbian Forbidden Erotica

Naked Twister: A Wild Party Game

Lexi: The Sex App (Lesbian Fantasy Erotica)

Call Girl: Lesbian Bisexual Threesomes Erotica

Circle Jill: Lesbian Masturbation Workshop

The Viewing Room: Masturbation Voyeur Erotica

Spin the Bottle: A Kinky Party Game

The Hair Salon: Lesbian Voyeur Erotica

Tribadism 1: Girls Only Sex Workshop

Tribadism 2: The Art of Scissoring

Tribadism 3: Threeway Hookups

The Kiss: A Game of Oral Sex

Pledge Week: Sorority Sisters

Carny Games 1: A Wild Sex Party

Carny Games 2: A Kinky Sex Party

Carny Games 3: An Erotic Sex Party

Dreamscape: An Artificial Reality Game

Glory Hole: Guess Who's On the Other Side

Joy Ride: A Late Night Erotic Bus Trip

The Blind Girl: An Erotic Romance(Coming Soon)

Lesbian Erotica Bundles:

Jade's Erotic Adventures: Books 1 - 5

Jade's Erotic Adventures: Books 6 - 10

Jade's Erotic Adventures: Books 11 - 15

Jade's Erotic Adventures: Books 16 - 20

Jade's Erotic Adventures: Books 21 - 25

Jade's Erotic Adventures: Books 26 - 30

Jade's Erotic Adventures: Books 31 - 35

Jade's Erotic Adventures: Books 36 - 40

Jade's Erotic Adventures: Books 41 - 45

Jade's Erotic Adventures: Books 46 - 50

Fifty Shades of Jade: Superbundle

Standalone Stories:

The Polynesian Girl: A Lesbian EroticRomance